The Lost Kitten

LEE · KOMAKO SAKAI

GECKO PRESS

When Hina and her mother opened the door, there was a skinny, scruffy kitten.

Behind it, a cat with two other kittens watched anxiously.

MEEeeeooow?

The cat bobbed her head as if saying, "Please look after my baby."

Hina and her mother were surprised. They had never been asked to do something by a cat before.

"Should we keep it?" Hina asked. "Its eyes are all gooey. What if it's dying?"

"That's why its mother brought it here," her mother answered. She looked up at the cat. "All right," she said. "We'll take care of it. Come and visit whenever you like."

The cat walked away.

"If we're going to have a kitten I'd rather get a cute one from the pet shop," Hina said. Her mother didn't reply.

She wet a soft towel and gently cleaned the kitten.
She wiped the goo from its eyes. They were big and blue,
and stared straight at Hina.

"It has beautiful eyes," Hina said.

"That's better," her mother told the kitten. "Tomorrow we'll take you to the vet."

"Can I touch it?"

"Yes. Gently though."

Hina stroked the kitten as gently as if she were touching butterfly wings.

The kitten seemed to like it.

Hina slipped her hand under its tummy and lifted.
It was so soft and light.

When she held the kitten, its tummy moved in and out and it purred deep in its throat.

"Even though it's so tiny," Hina said, "it's alive."

The kitten gave a little mew, as if saying goodbye to its mother.

Hina brought it inside.

It looked around and sniffed.

Hina's mother gave it some milk. The kitten lapped it up with its little tongue.

When it finished drinking, it walked around uncertainly then crept under the cupboard.

"It drank the milk. That's a good sign," Hina's mother said. "Let's leave it alone for a while until it gets used to us."

Hina's mother shredded newspaper for a litter box.

She put a towel in a cardboard box for its bed.

Hina slipped a little bell onto a ribbon to make a collar.

"I'd better go and buy some cat food. Grandma's resting in the other room if you need anything, Hina, but will you take care of the kitten?"

And Hina's mother rushed out the door.

While she was gone, Hina thought up names for the kitten.

Maybe Bluey for its eyes. Or Twiggy because it was so skinny. Teeny…Tiny Tim… But she didn't know if it was a girl or a boy.

Just thinking about the kitten made her happy.

She went to see how it was doing, but the kitten had disappeared.

"Kitty, where are you? Here, kitty-kitty."

Maybe it was frightened, being in a strange house.

Maybe it had run outside when Hina's mother opened the door.

What if it was lost?

Hina had been lost once.

She was in a store full of people and things she'd never seen before. She was holding onto what she thought was her mother's skirt.

But when she looked up, it wasn't her mother.

Hina burst into tears.

People gathered around her.

"What's your name?" "Where do you live?" they asked.

Someone took her hand and said, "It's okay, dear," and started walking.

Hina cried for her mother.

She thought she'd never see her mother again.
That was how the kitten must feel.

"The cat left us her kitten. Now I have to be its mother. I have to give it a name. I have to find it."

Hina began to search outside, pretending to be a kitten. "Meee, meeee, meeeeow."

She called and called, but there was no reply.

"Come on, kitty! I'll take care of you. I'll always be your friend. Here, kitty!"

Hina squeezed her eyes shut.

Whooooshh!

A cold wind shook the branches.

She looked up. The sun was setting.

She couldn't give up. She must find the kitten.

Hina hurried inside for her coat and a blanket to wrap the kitten in.

"Wait for me, kitty," she said.

But when she put on her coat…

… there was the kitten!

Just then, Hina's mother came home.

Hina was so relieved she began to cry.

When Hina stopped crying, her mother gently scooped up the kitten.

It looked so peaceful.

"It sleeps a lot," Hina said.
"Ah! I'll call it Sleepy!"

"Won't Grandma be surprised when we tell her," Hina's mother said with a smile.

Sleepy has been very fond of Hina's sweater ever since.

"Sleepy, let's be friends forever, okay?"

"Hey, stop sleeping so much. Are you listening, Sleepy?"

This edition first published in 2017 by Gecko Press
PO Box 9335, Marion Square, Wellington 6141, New Zealand
info@geckopress.com

English language edition © Gecko Press Ltd 2017

Original edition published in Japan by Bronze Publishing Inc., Tokyo, under the title
Yokuneru to Hina © 2015 LEE, Komako Sakai
English translation rights arranged with Bronze Publishing Inc., through Paper Crane Agency

All rights reserved. No part of this publication may be reproduced or transmitted or utilized
in any form, or by any means, electronic, mechanical, photocopying or otherwise without
the prior written permission of the publisher.

Distributed in the United States and Canada by Lerner Publishing Group, www.lernerbooks.com
Distributed in the United Kingdom by Bounce Sales and Marketing, www.bouncemarketing.co.uk
Distributed in Australia by Scholastic Australia, www.scholastic.com.au
Distributed in New Zealand by Upstart Distribution, www.upstartpress.co.nz

Translated by Cathy Hirano
Edited by Penelope Todd
Design and typesetting by Vida & Luke Kelly, New Zealand
Printed in Malaysia

ISBN hardback: 978-1-776571-26-0

For more curiously good books, visit www.geckopress.com